OLIVIA
and the Puppy Wedding

adapted by Tina Gallo
based on the screenplay "Puppy Love" written by Matt Negrete
illustrated by Patrick Spaziante

Simon Spotlight
New York   London   Toronto   Sydney   New Delhi

Based on the TV series *OLIVIA*™ as seen on Nickelodeon™

SIMON SPOTLIGHT
An imprint of Simon & Schuster Children's Publishing Division
1230 Avenue of the Americas, New York, New York 10020
OLIVIA TM Ian Falconer Ink Unlimited, Inc. and ©2012 Ian Falconer and Classic Media, LLC
For information about special discounts for bulk purchases, please contact
Simon & Schuster Special Sales at 1-866-506-1949 or
business@simonandschuster.com.
Manufactured in the United States of America 0712 LAK
1 2 3 4 5 6 7 8 9 10 First Edition
ISBN 978-1-4424-5315-9 (pbk)
ISBN 978-1-4424-5316-6 (eBook)

Olivia was helping her mom plan a wedding reception. "Planning a wedding is fun, Mom," Olivia said. "What else can I do to help?"

"Why don't you play with Perry while I take these invitations to the mailbox?" Mom said.

"Hmm," Olivia answered. "What if I take the invitations to the mailbox, and take Perry with me?"

Olivia walked down to the mailbox, singing a happy tune.
"*Wedding groom and wedding bride,*" Olivia sang.
Perry howled.
"Great singing, Perry!" Olivia said, and Perry howled again.

Olivia dropped all the wedding invitations into the mailbox. She kept singing, and so did Perry!

But suddenly it sounded as if there were two dogs singing!

Perry began running, pulling Olivia with him. Perry stopped short.

Olivia crashed into Perry, who was playing with another dog.

"Perry, you made a new friend!" Olivia said. "What's your name?"
Perry's new friend barked.
"Did you say 'Cherry'?" Olivia asked her.
The dog barked again.
Olivia smiled. "It was nice meeting you, Cherry, but Perry and I need to get home. See you later!"

"Hi, Mom. I'm back!" Olivia shouted as she entered her house. Mom looked past Olivia with surprise. "Oh! And you brought company?"

Olivia turned around and saw Cherry.

"Did she follow you home?" Mom asked.

"Actually I think she followed Perry home," Olivia said. "I think they're in love."

"She doesn't have a collar," Mom said. "How did you know her name was Cherry?"

"She told me!" Olivia said.

"Oh, of course," Mom answered. "But with no collar, it's going to be difficult to find her home. Why don't you play outside with the dogs while I start making calls to find her owner?"

Perry and Cherry looked so cute together, Olivia took a picture of
them.
Perry barked at Olivia.
"What did you say, Perry?" Olivia asked. "You want to get married?
And you want me to plan it? Well, I do have a way with animals. But
I'll need some help."

Olivia called Francine to ask for her help planning the wedding.
"A doggie wedding?" Francine asked. "With bouquets and
decorations and wedding guests?"
"Yes!" Olivia answered. "But we can't have guests without invitations."
Olivia began looking for supplies in her trunk.
"Let's see . . . fancy red ribbon . . . paper . . . doggie bones.
Perfect!"

Francine and Olivia handed out invitations to all their friends and classmates. Olivia handed her teacher an invitation. Mrs. Hoggenmuller was thrilled.

"How delightful!" she said. She looked at her two cats. "Can I bring a guest . . . or two?"

"Of course!" Olivia answered. "The more the merrier!"

Soon Olivia had only one invitation left. She went to her friend
Daisy's house to deliver it.
"Hi, Daisy!" Olivia said. "My dog, Perry, is getting married today.
Want to come to the wedding?"
"I can't go to a silly wedding," Daisy said. "I've lost something really
important, and I have to find it!"
She shut the door. Olivia was surprised.
"Who said it was silly?" she asked Francine.

Back at Olivia's house Francine and Olivia looked at pictures in a bridal magazine.

"This magazine says brides like bows and veils," Francine told Olivia.

A few minutes later Cherry was wearing a bridal outfit.

"I used a pink napkin for her veil, and added a big red bow," Olivia explained.

"Ohhh, she's beautiful!" Francine said.

Soon it was time for the big event!

"Hello, wedding guest people!" Ian said. "The wedding will start in exactly . . . pretty soon."

"Olivia?" Francine asked. "Where did Cherry go?"

Olivia was surprised. "She was just here a minute ago!" she said. "We have to find her!"

Olivia and Francine were looking for Cherry when the doorbell rang. It was Daisy, and she didn't look happy. "After looking for my missing dog all day, I opened up your wedding invitation and saw my missing dog!"

"Well, Daisy, I have good news and bad news," Olivia said. "The good news is that your dog is getting married. The bad news is . . . she ran away. But don't worry, we'll find her!"

Olivia and Daisy ran outside calling for the missing bride-to-be.

"Cherry!" Olivia called.

"Miss Buttercup!" Daisy called.

"You named my dog Cherry?" Daisy said.

"You named your dog Miss Buttercup?" Olivia said.

Daisy nodded and stared at Olivia.

"I like it!" Olivia said.

After a while Daisy was ready to give up.

"It's no use, she could be anywhere," Daisy said sadly.

At that moment both girls heard Perry howling.

Olivia smiled. "That's it! Daisy, I know how to find Cherry—I mean Miss Buttercup! Come on!"

"The only sound Miss Buttercup likes better than Perry singing is the sound of both of us singing together," Olivia explained.

Olivia began to sing. Perry howled and sang along.

After a minute or two they heard another dog's faraway howl.

Olivia listened carefully. "It's Miss Buttercup!" she said.

"It sounds like she's by the mailbox!"

Olivia and Daisy peeked behind the mailbox, and there was the runaway bride!

"You put a bow on her head?" Daisy said. "No wonder she ran away. She hates bows! Thanks for finding her, Olivia. But I still don't want her to marry your dog."

Daisy opened her arms wide. "Hi, Miss Buttercup! Come to Mama!"
But Miss Buttercup ignored Daisy and ran straight to Perry.
Olivia smiled. "Daisy, are you sure you don't want to let your dog
marry Perry?"

It was time for the wedding. Olivia stood beside Perry and Miss Buttercup. She looked at Daisy.
"So, if Daisy says it's okay . . ."
Daisy opened her mouth to speak.

Olivia started talking very quickly. "Daisy already gave her permission. I heard her. So, I now pronounce you doggie and wife!" Olivia said. "Perry, you may kiss the bride!"

Daisy smiled at her dog. "I guess I should call you *Mrs.* Buttercup now," she said.

"You did a great job planning your doggie wedding today, Olivia," Mom said.

At that moment Perry hopped onto Olivia's bed and whimpered.

"What's that, Perry? You want me to plan your honeymoon?" Olivia said.

Mom smiled. "That can wait until tomorrow. Good night, Olivia."

"Good night, Mom. I have so much to do," Olivia said with a yawn.

Soon she was fast asleep.